W9-BUH-807

FLYING FURBALLS
Dogfight

DONOVAN BIXLEY

upstart press

In memory of C4 and Syd, two beloved furballs.

Approved by SPoCA (The Society for the
Protection of Cartoon Animals). No pets were
harmed in the drawing of this book.

A catalogue record for this book is available from the
National Library of New Zealand

ISBN 978-1-927262-53-5

An Upstart Press Book
Published in 2016 by Upstart Press Ltd
B3, 72 Apollo Drive, Rosedale
Auckland, New Zealand

Reprinted 2016

Text and illustrations © Donovan Bixley 2016
The moral rights of the author have been asserted.

All rights reserved. No part of this publication may be
reproduced or transmitted in any form or by any means,
electronic or mechanical, including photocopying,
recording, or any information storage and retrieval system,
without permission in writing from the publisher.

Printed by 1010 Printing International Limited, China

R0448474093

MEET SOME OF THE CHARACTERS AT CATs HQ

Claude D'Bonair is the youngest pilot in the CATs Air Corps. He may be small, but his bravery and quick cat cunning have helped him survive many dangerous missions.

Syd Fishus flew the first airplanes with Claude's father before the war. He was once the most dashing pilot in katdom, but he has a fondness for kippers and cream . . . and a few other bad habits.

Manx is never happier than when she has a wrench in her hand and something to fix. It's a busy job, but CATs' head mechanic also has to keep an eye out for her two sisters: fidgeting **Wigglebum**, and ever-curious **Picklepurr**.

Major Ginger Tom is the most famous pilot in all of katdom . . . and he knows it!

C-for is HQ's resident inventor, forever dreaming up crazy new gadgets for the pilots to try out.

Commander Katerina Snookums is the head of CATs Air Corps. **General Fluffington** is her right-hand man, along with his secretary, **Mr Tiddles**.

Sinja and **Mitzi** are nurses with CATs Medical Corps.

Mrs Cushion is never far from the action with her tea trolley.

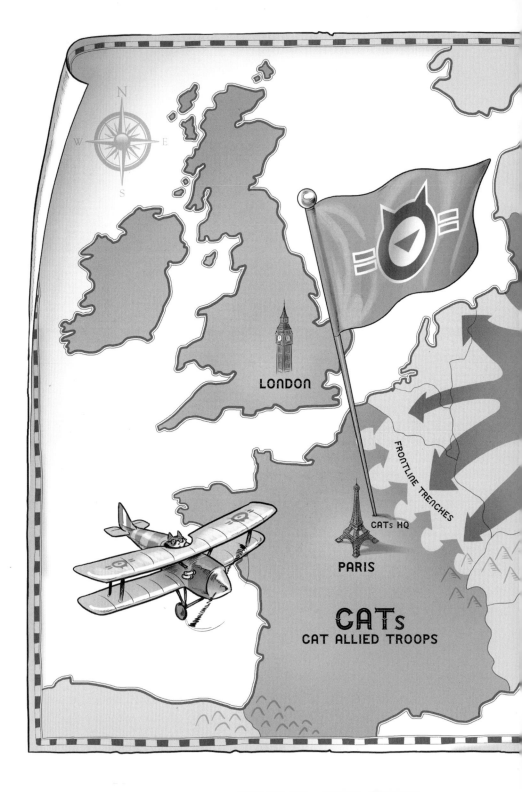

BERLIN

DOGZ
DOG OBEDIENCE
GOVERNED ZONE

EUROPE 1916

A great war is under way. Cats and dogs once
lived together in peace. That was before a pack
calling themselves DOGZ took over the kingdoms
of Central Europe. As the invading DOGZ army
advances on Paris, the Cat Allied Troops (CATs)
have gathered from every corner of the katdom to
save Europe from going to the DOGZ.

CHATEAU FUR-DE-LYS

CATs headquarters (HQ) on the outskirts of Paris.
Over 300 years old, the palace was used as an art
gallery before the war.

1. City of Paris
2. Chateau woodlands
3. Workshop scrap-heap
4. Aircraft hangars and workshop in former stables
5. Airstrip
6. Reflection pond
7. Secret Base Command in the chateau's catacombs
8. Gazebo, includes secret entrance to Base Command
9. West wing, pilots' quarters
10. Air traffic control tower in turret
11. Top floors, used by Commander Snookums and her staff
12. Hedge maze
13. Ornamental gardens
14. East wing, Medical Corps
15. Guard-house

CHAPTER 1

'Flying furballs!' blurted Claude D'Bonair.

'Steady on, young airman,' said General Fluffington. 'There's no need for rough language.'

'But sir,' said Claude, 'you've just told us that the DOGZ are planning some dastardly new attack.'

General Fluffington shook his hairy head. 'It's true, but I'm afraid I have worse news still.'

The top pilots from Cat Allied Troops, or CATs as it was known, had been summoned to a meeting at their secret underground headquarters with Commander Katerina Snookums, General Fluffington, and Mr Tiddles, the General's secretary.

'You see,' the General went on, 'one of our pilots has gone missing over enemy territory.' He pointed to a big map on the wall.

Syd Fishus snorted. 'No worries, General,' he said, patting his round belly. 'Any cat worth his wings will find their way home at the sound of the dinner bell.' Syd was old enough to have flown with Claude's father, and he was as round as Santa Claws.

'Not every cat is obsessed with kippers and cream,' quipped Mr Tiddles from behind his desk.

'True, mate,' said Syd. 'And some of us risk our lives every day in the airforce, not safe at HQ in the *chairforce*.' He turned to Claude in the seat next to him. 'And I'm not *obsessed* with kippers and cream. Sometimes I could really go for lobster and cream.'

Claude just laughed. He knew that Syd had once been an ace pilot, and Claude was sure there was still much he could pick up from the old cat — though not any of his bad habits.

Syd leaned back and puffed on his pipe of catnip. 'So,' he said, 'what silly young kit has forgotten how to read their navigation charts this time?'

'That's the bad news,' said Commander Snookums. 'I'm afraid it wasn't just some silly young pilot.'

She let out a huff of breath. 'It was Major Ginger Tom.'

There was a gasp from the assembled pilots.

'Crikey dingo!' swore Syd.

Everyone knew that Major Tom was the top dogfighter in the whole katdom. Young kits had their

bedroom walls plastered with his dashing pictures, cut from his many appearances in the newspapers. Only the previous week Major Tom had single-handedly derailed an enemy train loaded with tons of dog roll. The attack had broken the DOGZ supply chain for weeks.

'Needless to say,' said General Fluffington gravely, 'this information is super-duper, extra-special, tippity-top secret, with sardines on top. If the public found out that their beloved hero was missing, the whole katdom might fall into despair. This news could bring down the entire war effort. Therefore, not a word is to leave this room.'

At that moment the tea lady rolled in with her trolley.

'For kitty's sake, Mrs Cushion!' the General roared. 'We're in the middle of a super-duper, extra-special, tippity-top secret meeting.'

'Don't forget the sardines on top,' said Syd, licking his lips.

Mrs Cushion backed out again without even stopping. Her trolley wheels could be heard squeak-squeaking away down the corridor like little mice.

Commander Snookums drew everyone's attention back to the map. She pulled out her pointer and extended it, then extended it again, and then had to extend it one more time to circle an area high up on the map. 'Major Ginger Tom was flying a secret mission for us over this region. The DOGZ have it defended with Howlitzer cannons and heavy machine

guns, so we haven't got any details of the terrain. We want to know what they're up to in there.'

'Probably licking their privates, ma'am,' said Syd, laughing with the other pilots.

Commander Snookums shot everyone a disapproving frown, and they fell silent. 'We are now certain that the Major was shot down and captured.

The DOGZ will want to find out everything that he knows, and it won't be long before they begin to torture him.'

'But Major Tom would never tell them anything!' exclaimed Claude. 'He's one of our top officers. He's trained to resist the DOGZ interrogation.'

'Look, mate,' said Syd. 'Us old pilots know it's only a matter of time. And when Major Tom cracks they'll have him wearing a collar and eating dog roll like it's catnip. When that happens, he'll tell them anything they want to know.'

'Including all our top military secrets,' said General Fluffington. 'It could spell catastrophe for all of us.'

'But what will they do to him?' asked Claude.

'I dunno,' said Syd, 'but I've heard the DOGZ have got a room that's big enough to swing a cat in.'

'No!' gasped Claude. 'They couldn't be that cruel! Not all dogs are DOGZ. Surely they can't all be bad?'

'Don't be a fool, young pilot,' said General Fluffington. 'They'll always be a bad bunch. You can't teach an old dog new tricks. But one thing's for certain, we must rescue Major Tom before it's too late. It'll be a difficult and dangerous mission, deep into the heart of DOGZ territory.'

Claude was first on his feet to volunteer. Syd made a show of refilling his pipe and looking uninterested.

'You're a credit to your squadron, Claude D'Bonair,' said the General, placing a heavy paw on Claude's shoulder. 'I'm sure your father would be proud. But unfortunately there are two problems. You see, we have no idea where Major Tom is being held. First, we must discover where the DOGZ have taken him. Secondly, young Claude, I think you have forgotten what happened at the end of your last mission . . .'

CHAPTER 2

'**C**rikey dingo!' said Syd, 'you really made a dog's dinner out of her this time.'

Syd and Claude were standing in a patch of open sunlight that poured through the big hangar doors, where the remains of Claude's plane were stored.

Syd took a puff on his catnip. 'What in the name of kitty litter did you do to her?'

'I was flying a routine patrol
over the front lines,' Claude
began. 'There wasn't a cloud in
the sky when he got me.'
  'Who?'

'I don't know who he was, but he was good. Flew straight out of the glaring sun, where I couldn't see him, gunning for me in his bright red plane.'

'Strewth, mate, that'll be The Red Setter. Did he have a great big K9 emblazoned across his plane?'

Claude nodded.

'That's The Red Setter then. He's the DOGZ poster boy – the most dangerous pilot they have. You're lucky to be alive.'

'I don't think it was luck,' said Claude.

'Oooh-weee,' purred Syd. 'This young kit thinks he's a flying ace like Major Tom!'

'No, I don't mean that,' said Claude. 'You see, he was right on my tail and his was the superior plane by far. All the while I was losing altitude and he was gaining the advantage. The thing is, there were plenty of times when he could have shot me out of the sky – but he didn't. I think he was only aiming for the plane and not wanting to shoot the pilot. *That's* why I'm still alive.'

'No chance, mate. Those dirty DOGZ

are all the same. Didn't you hear what General Fluffington said?'

'Hmmm,' murmured Claude. 'Well, eventually I tried to make a dash for it, and he let off a burst of gunfire which took out my engine. I fought with the controls like a thrashing eel, and I managed to bring her back to our side. The red plane—'

'The Red Setter . . .'

'Yes, The Red Setter took off when our ground troops started taking pot-shots at him. I crash-landed in a field of catnip.'

'Crikey no!'

'It's okay,' said Claude. 'I got out before the plane caught fire.'

'Not you! All that wasted catnip,' moaned Syd. 'Oh well, you'll be grounded for months now.'

A voice came from the shadows of the hangar. 'Only a week or two if I can help it.' A white cat strode into the light.

'Manx!' grinned Claude.

She wiped her paws on an oily rag and shoved it in her overalls before giving Claude a friendly punch on the shoulder.

Syd coughed smoke out of his nose. 'You're not gonna let this . . . this *girl* fix your kite are you, Claude?'

'Sure thing,' said Claude, clapping her around the shoulders. 'Manx is the best in the business.'

'Learnt everything I know from me old dad,' she grinned.

Just then two small furballs came flying across the hangar and collided with Claude. He looked down to see two kittens clinging to his legs. 'Wigglebum! Picklepurr!' laughed Claude, trying to shake them off.

'Leave Claude alone, you two,' said Manx. 'Come on, off with you now. You're both such mischief-makers and I don't want you getting filthy in the hangar. Goodness, what would mother and father think if they were here!'

Manx sent her two younger sisters scampering away, and walked around the wrecked plane with Claude, pointing out all the modifications she was planning.

'See, she's a bit old-fashioned,' said Manx.

'Nothin' wrong with old,' said Syd tagging along behind. '*Old* is just another word for *experienced*.'

'Well then,' laughed Manx, running her paw along a crumpled wing. 'This plane has had a *lot* of experience. Look Claude, technology has advanced since she was made. But if I pull back the angle of the wings, make some adjustments to the rudder, and overhaul the engine, she'll be the best plane in the skies. Of course it'll make her a bit unstable and harder to take off and land. But once she's in the air, she'll turn on a pinhead. Don't you agree, Syd?'

'Oh, I dunno nothin' about any of that. I'm just an ace flyer.'

'More like an ace *fryer*, from the size of your belly.'

'Hey!' growled Syd.

'When can you get started?' asked Claude.

'Straight away.'

'Fantastic! The sooner the better. See Syd, I told you she was the best.'

But Syd was looking the other way.

'Well hell-ooo kitties,' purred Syd.

Claude turned around to see Sinja and Mitzi, two nurses from the Medical Corps, passing by the hangar door. Syd went over and wrapped an arm around each of them.

When they saw Claude, they wriggled free of
Syd's big paws and flounced over.

'Hi Claude,' said Mitzi, ignoring Manx. 'Don't
you look handsome in your uniform.'

Sinja cast a disdainful eye over
Manx. 'It's so dirty in here,' she
sneered. 'Just the smell makes my
whiskers twitch.' Manx rolled her
eyes and stalked off to work on
Claude's wrecked plane.

'Manx!' Claude called after her.
'We'll talk later, okay?'

'Ewww,' said Sinja, not even
lowering her voice. 'Did you see that?
She doesn't even have a tail.'

'How awful for her,' said Mitzi.

'Awful's the word alright!' giggled
Sinja. 'And what about those greasy overalls.
What kind of feline would ever let herself wear
those in public?'

'Now girls, no need to be catty,' said Syd.

'Oh, we're just having some fun,' said Sinja.

'Yes Syd, it's our day off and we're sooooo bored,' said Mitzi. 'We tried sleeping all day but we were even too bored for that. We were so bored we even had to go for a walk — *outdoors!*'

'Oh Syd, please take us for a drive into Paris in your new car,' they whined. 'It would be just purr-fect.'

'Geez, I dunno, girls.'

'But Syd, you're so big and stwong,' said Sinja.

'Well, I do have an especially hearty appetite,' Syd chuckled.

'You really fill out that uniform.'

He sure does, thought Claude with a grin.

'Plenty of me to go around, ladies,' laughed Syd. 'Well? Are you all coming to Paris with me or not?'

Claude sighed and looked back at the wreck of his plane. 'It's not *going* anywhere,' giggled Sinja. *Just like our plans to rescue Major Tom,* thought Claude. Sinja grabbed Claude's arm and dragged him away.

CHAPTER

'No cream?!' roared Syd.

They were sitting in one of the fashionable street cafés in Paris, with a beautiful view of the Eiffel Tower. All around were dozens of other army officers and soldiers, sent back from the front lines for a few days of rest and recreation in the city of love. None of them looked as swish as the two airmen and the beautiful nurses.

'Why don't you just have a milk?' said Claude, trying to calm Syd.

'Milk!' snorted Syd. 'Look, mate, every day I risk my bleedin' life for the katdom and all I ask in return is a pipe of catnip, a plate of kippers, and a nice cold glass of cream.'

'Have you forgotten? The war has caused a lot of shortages,' Claude reminded him. 'Besides, it's only noon. Far too early to be drinking cream.'

'Oh, Syd knows how to have fun any time

of day,' giggled Mitzi.

An elegant Siamese cat came over and Syd asked the nurses what they'd like to order. The Siamese cat slipped Claude a note and walked off.

'How rude!' huffed Sinja.

Claude unfolded the note. 'She wants us to follow her,' he said to Syd. He leaped up, dragging Syd with him.

'How rude!' huffed Mitzi.

The two airmen made their way through the café. Diners chatted and the cutlery clinked on china plates. They saw the Siamese cat head through a door out to the kitchen. As they passed the counter Claude had to drag Syd away from the stacks of exquisite cat biscuits stacked under large glass domes.

They followed the cat into
the kitchens, and were hit by
an array of wonderful aromas.

'Ooooh I've got a good feeling
about this,' purred Syd. 'Maybe she
wants us to sample her new menu?'

One of the chefs slapped Syd's paw away from a
steaming fish pie.

'Come on,' scowled Claude.

The Siamese cat was
waiting for them at the
back door. She indicated
that the two pilots should
go through, and they
entered an alleyway.

A small figure emerged from the shadows, wrapped in a long trench coat. His hat was pulled down over his face, but the two cats sniffed trouble in an instant.

The figure reached into his jacket. 'It's a trap!'
cried Syd, pouncing forward.

Syd's huge bulk collided with the small figure, knocking off the hat — and revealing the dog disguised beneath. There was a brief scuffle and a loud crack.

When the dust settled, Syd was sitting on top of the little dog.

'Are you okay?' asked Claude.

'It's alright,' grinned Syd. 'I'm fine.'

'Not you!' said Claude. 'Hop off him, you great lump.'

A groan came from underneath Syd. 'I think I broke my tail.'

Claude helped the little dog to his feet.

'Sorry about my friend. He smokes too much catnip.'

'That's the thanks I get for saving your bacon?'

'It wasn't a gun, you big furball,' said Claude. And when Syd looked again he saw that the little dog had not pulled a gun out of his jacket, but an envelope.

'I've been waiting back here for hours,' said the dog. 'Waiting for some CATs airmen, such as you, to come into Yuki's café.' He indicated the Siamese cat by the door.

'Yuki is a very brave cat,' he went on. 'She helped disguise me and smuggle me across the front lines into Paris.' He looked Claude deep in the eyes. 'Please believe me when I say that not all dogs are DOGZ.'

He pressed the envelope into Claude's paw. 'I am sure you will find the information in this envelope very interesting. But now I must go, it's too dangerous to stay here. If either side caught me . . .' He let the words trail off.

'Too blimmin' right, mate!' said Syd. 'Let's nab the little mongrel and take him in to HQ for questioning.'

'No,' said Claude, holding Syd back. 'I think we can trust this dog. Besides, we're already in trouble. How would we ever explain what we were doing talking to a dog in the first place? We'd be cat-martialled for sure.'

When they turned back, the dog had already sped down the alleyway. 'What's your name?' Claude called after him.

The dog stopped at the end of the alley and thought for a second. 'You can call me Rex,' he said, before disappearing into the shadows.

'What is this codswallop?' said Syd. He and Claude were back at HQ in their barracks, trying to make sense of the information that the little dog Rex had given them in the envelope. 'It's revolting DOGZ propaganda,' Syd went on. 'And it's no blimmin' use to us. I say we go straight to Commander Snookums and tell her about our little meeting with the spying dog.
In no time our troops
will be scouring Paris
for that mangey mongrel.
Rex indeed!'

Syd clawed the note and
screwed it into a tight ball.

'No, wait!' said Claude.
'I think, I was almost on to
something.' He took the note
and flattened it out.

Message To All faithful followers of The Supreme leader of dogs, and soon, the lesser species of Cats.

Hold fast to our dear Leader alf alpha, Our furrer who Shows us the way, our faithful guide dog.

Sacrifices have to be made, but Soon across all the Lands, all dogs and cats will swear Obedience to the furrer.

Before long we will live in a Better Europe Ruled entirely by dogs, where Cats know their place and Hand Over their lands, their rights, and their Possessions to dogs!

'Look here!' Claude ran his claw over the note. 'These capital letters are unusual. I think it's a message. Yes. Can you see it? Take the capitals and put them together. What do you get?'

Syd scrunched up his face trying to read it. 'Uhhhh . . . MTATSCH LOSSS LOB BERCHOP? What in dog's name is that supposed to mean?'

'No, like this,' said Claude. 'MT AT SCHLOSS SLOBBERCHOP.'

'Schloss Slobberchop?' said Syd.

'Schloss is a castle,' explained Claude.

'I know what a Schloss is, you young kit!' snapped Syd. 'But what does MT mean?'

'Major Tom — MT,' said Claude.

'Of course,' said Syd. 'And what's Slobberchop?'

'That must be the name of the castle.'

'Ah, of course, it all makes sense now . . . so what does the AT stand for?'

'It means that Major Tom is being held prisoner AT Castle Slobberchop. Thanks to Rex we now have the information we need to rescue Major Tom.'

'What did I tell you, Claude,' said Syd, snatching up the note. 'I knew that little dog was on our side all along. Quick, let's get this to General Fluffington.'

'Hold on!' said Claude. 'There might be all sorts of questions about where we got this information. You know what the General thinks about dogs.'

'You're right,' said Syd, loading his pipe with fresh catnip. 'We can't let anyone know that we've been chatting in dark alleys with dogs or we'll be kicked out of the air corps—' Syd gulped, 'or worse! Best we keep this mission our little secret, I reckon.'

'Did I hear secret mission?' came a creaking voice behind them. Syd and Claude nearly jumped out of their fur. They spun around to see old C-for hunched in the doorway. He pushed his glasses back up his nose and said, 'I was just passing in the corridor and couldn't help overhearing. Yes, I've got just the thing for you. I've been waiting for the right airmen to go on a dangerous secret mission.'

'Secret misson?' said Claude. 'Ahhh . . . no . . .

we're not going on any secret mission.'

'Yes, you're completely right,' said C-for. 'Hurry up you two. No time to lose.'

CHAPTER 5

C-for's workshop was a mess of machinery and tools, with half-made contraptions lying everywhere. On the walls hung some of his more successful inventions: the remote-control dog collar, the radio transmitter cat biscuit, and the exploding fake dog poop.

C-for had curled up asleep at his workbench as soon as they had arrived.

Syd snorted. 'Let's get out of here before the old coot wakes up.'

Just then the old coot woke up with a start. 'Hmph. What? Yes, you're completely right. Now what was I doing?'

'You were just sleeping,' said Syd.

'Just sleeping? *Just* sleeping? I'll have you know that I come up with some of my best ideas when I'm asleep.'

Claude and Syd exchanged doubtful glances.

'At any rate, this is what I wanted to give you.' C-for opened a drawer and pulled out his latest invention.

'But I already have a watch,' said Claude.

'Foolish young kit,' snapped C-for. 'This is no ordinary watch. For a start it doesn't even tell the time.'

'Good watch then,' scoffed Syd.

'If you stop interrupting I'll tell you what it does. See . . . press this button and it fires a high-strength micro-wire with a barb on the end that will hook into any material. Then another press of the button and it will winch you up in a jiffy. You adjust the hands on the watch face to set the length of wire you need. So 3 o'clock fires out 3 metres of wire, 6 o'clock fires 6 metres, and so on around the clock.'

WINCH–WATCH

1. Set button. Adjusts the hand
2. Watch face. The hand indicates how many metres of micro-wire will fire. Watch is currently set to 2 metres
3. High-strength micro-wire. Maximum length 12 metres
4. Toughened steel tip. Barb will embed in any material
5. Intricate winch mechanism has been designed to fit inside a wrist-watch
6. Activate button. Press to fire. Press again to winch in

OPERATION

How to scale a high wall

Set and aim   Fire   Activate winch

'How come he gets the fancy gadgets?' complained Syd.

'I'm afraid I had to make some modifications to fit the mechanism into a watch. One limitation was the weight it can lift. If I was to make one big enough to lift you, Syd, you might as well carry a grandfather clock on your back.'

Claude slipped the watch on his wrist.

'Careful, young whippersnapper!' said C-for. 'Don't point that thing at me. You'll cause all manner of mayhem if you fire it indoors. Now I only have one important instruction,' said C-for. 'Whatever you do, don't—'

'Yes?' said Claude. 'Don't what?'

But C-for was already fast asleep again.

CHAPTER 6

Syd and Claude waited until midnight before they sneaked out to the aircraft hangars. Syd had found a map which showed the location of Schloss Slobberchop deep in the heart of DOGZ country. It was an old pre-war map, so unfortunately it didn't show any of the command posts now heavily defended by the DOGZ.

The two cats did not even know if they could
trust Rex or Yuki, the café owner. If it all went wrong
and HQ found out that they had been secretly
meeting with a dog, they would really be in the
doghouse. Claude consoled himself that if it *was*
a trap designed to lure the entire CATs Air Corps
within range of the DOGZ guns, at least only two of
them would die.

However, if it all went according to plan and they
rescued Major Tom . . . well, then he and Syd would
be front-page news across all of katdom.

The plan was simple. After landing in an open
area of forest, Claude would use his winch-watch to
scale the castle walls. Next they'd find Major Tom,
and then they would all run like mad. They were
confident that any cats worth their flea powder
should be able to lose a few dogs once they were in
the forest. Then they would leap back into the plane
and be home in time to have kippers for breakfast.

They were eyeing a powerful new two-seater
aircraft that had enough firepower to take on the

entire DOGZ airforce. 'This'll do the job perfectly,' purred Claude.

'Oh no you don't!' said a voice from the darkness. The game was up. They had been caught before their plan had even got off the ground.

But it wasn't the military police.

'I've got a better plane you can use,' said the
figure. Claude's eyes slowly adjusted to the dark.

'Manx!' he cheered.

'What a rusting pile of junk!' said Syd.

Manx, Claude and Syd stood amongst a pile of
scraps and airplane parts that littered the airfield
behind the hangars. The moon peeked out from
behind the clouds, illuminating an outdated old
bi-plane.

'It's a Morane-Saulnier BB,' said Manx.

MORANE-SAULNIER TYPE BB

(1) Tail rudder steers the plane left and right

(2) Tail elevators steer the plane up and down

(3) Lewis gun fires 600 rounds (bullets) per minute

(4) Magazine holds 97 x 0.303 rounds (enough for only 10 seconds of continuous firing)

(5) Passenger/gunner seat

(6) Pilot's cockpit and controls (see inset)

(7) Fuselage — made of wood and canvas

(8) Ailerons on each wing help roll the plane to the left or right

(9) Wings. Early planes had multiple wings because designers were still experimenting with what worked and what didn't. Some planes had five sets of wings or more!

(10) 110 horsepower engine — equivalent to 550 dogpower. Produces top speed of 150 km/hr

(11) Engine exhaust pipes

(12) Wooden propeller blades. Early aircraft didn't have a starter motor. The pilot would flick the magneto switches and the ground crew had to yank hard on the propeller to start the engine running. A deadly job if you didn't get out of the way quickly

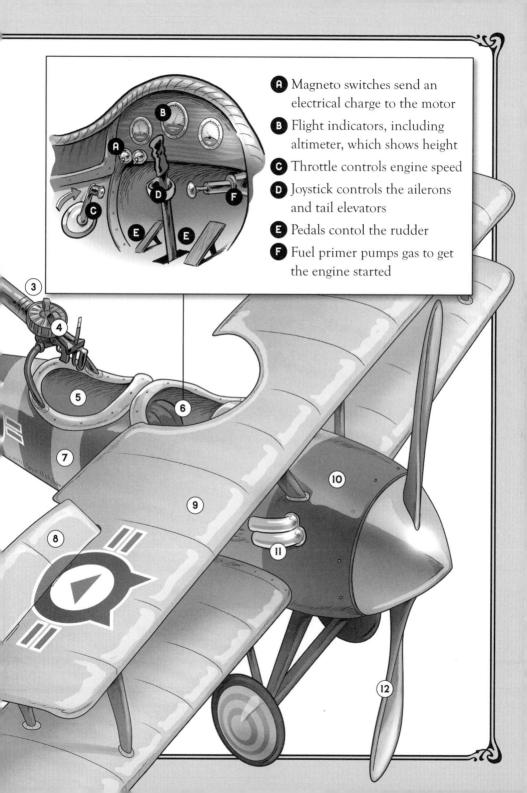

A Magneto switches send an electrical charge to the motor

B Flight indicators, including altimeter, which shows height

C Throttle controls engine speed

D Joystick controls the ailerons and tail elevators

E Pedals contol the rudder

F Fuel primer pumps gas to get the engine started

'I rebuilt her from scrap parts we had lying around the yard,' said Manx. 'She doesn't look pretty but she's a solid scout plane — if a little out of date. She has some benefits though. First of all, she belongs to me. So when your plan goes horribly wrong, at least you won't be charged with stealing a military aircraft.'

'Oh, you're a barrel of confidence,' snorted Syd.

Manx ignored him. 'Secondly, she's full of gas. I've also fixed a brand-new rear-mounted Lewis machine gun to the back seat. You won't be able to attack, but if anything's behind you this gun will shred it to pieces.'

Claude gave an admiring whistle.

'Well, you never know when *these* kind of emergencies are going to pop up,' grinned Manx.

'Anything else?' asked Syd.

'She's already out here on the airstrip. I don't know what you were planning, but you two idiots would have made a great ballyhoo just opening the hangar doors. You'd have been caught in seconds.'

Syd scowled, but Claude just chuckled.

Manx really was worth a dozen cats.

'What are you two doing here?' said Manx,
looking past the two pilots.
They turned to find Picklepurr
and Wigglebum yawning in
their pyjamas.

'We heard you get up and
wanted to see what was going
on,' said curious Pickle.

'Well, you've seen enough
excitement for one night,' said
Manx, and she shooed them off to bed.

Claude leaped up into the catpit, and began
tweaking the controls. Instantly there was a
horrible noise.

Claude shot Manx a worried look. *Was this plane
even going to start?*

'Doggone it!' swore Syd. *He* was the thing that was wheezing and grunting as he tried to squeeze his fat belly into the gunner's seat. His rolls of flesh were bulging up over the sides like an overflowing bowl of jellymeat. 'Airmen must have been smaller in the old days,' complained Syd. 'Not as . . . *muscular* as we are today.'

Manx rolled her eyes. 'I guess I could make some alterations by morning.'

'We've no time,' growled Syd, slapping his paw on the side of the fuselage. It gave a rattling jiggle that made his belly wobble. 'Every minute lost is a minute that Major Tom is being tortured. We must act now before all of CATs' plans are known to the DOGZ.'

Syd hauled himself out of the gunner's seat. 'I'm sorry young cobber, but you're going to have to go it alone.'

'There's no time to lose,' said Claude.

As soon as Syd jumped down, Claude pumped the fuel primer then threw the magneto switches. Manx heaved on the propeller, starting the engine. The motor coughed and spluttered, belching out a cloud of smoke, before roaring to life.

'Good luck!' shouted Manx. 'Come back in one piece.'

'I'll do my best!' Claude yelled back.

'Hey Claude!' bellowed Syd. 'When the reporters come, don't leave me out of the story.'

Claude laughed and gunned the throttle.

Within minutes he was a dark speck against the moon, before turning the plane east and heading towards DOGZ country — and into more danger than he could possibly imagine.

CHAPTER  7

The engine droned as the little Morane-Saulnier BB chugged along. Every once in a while Claude thought he heard a high-pitched whining coming from the plane, but then it would stop. Down below, the farms and fields were bathed in a glow of bluish moonlight.

Claude had to fly at high altitude, where he wouldn't be heard or seen. Up here the wind was freezing. He pulled his scarf tight around his face to stop icicles forming on his whiskers.

Claude had memorised Syd's map, as he couldn't be pulling it out every few minutes while he was flying. He headed east, keeping the North Star to his left at 9 o'clock.

Airmen use the hands on a clock to describe direction in relation to their plane.

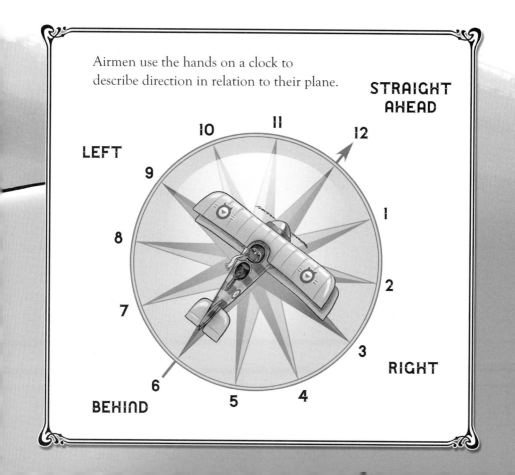

STRAIGHT AHEAD

LEFT

12

11

10

9

1

8

2

7

3

RIGHT

6

5

4

BEHIND

Soon he could see, far far below, the moon shining on the front lines where the ground battle between the CATs and the invading DOGZ army was being fought. The wide fields and farms gave way to barren, dead lands of broken trees, mud and rubble. Claude could see the destruction caused by the battle. He suddenly felt like he was flying over the pitted surface of the moon, not the once-lush fields of France.

Not far from the CATs trenches, he flew over the positions where the DOGZ had dug themselves in.

And just like that, he was in enemy territory.

Without a map, Claude was on the lookout for the next clue that would guide him to Schloss Slobberchop, all the while staying alert for enemy fighters. Within minutes he came across what he was looking for. The land ahead was swallowed up by a deep black forest, and running through it, like a ribbon of silver in the moonlight, was a wide river. Claude simply had to follow the river until he came across the castle, then scout for a place to land. 'Hmph, that's if the plane will make it,' muttered Claude. He could hear that whining noise again.

Below were towns and villages, lit up with orange lights and bustling with DOGZ activity. The roads were busy with traffic, despite it being the middle of the night. Even with his sharp cat eyesight he couldn't make out what was going on from this high altitude. As much as his curiosity ached to see what the DOGZ were up to, he didn't want to risk a low pass. The DOGZ might hear his engine and shoot him down. He reminded himself that curiosity killed the cat. Commander Snookums had been right, the DOGZ were definitely up to something, and Claude would have to remember all the details to tell HQ — *if* he got back with all nine lives intact. Right now he had to focus on his mission and the rescue of Major Ginger Tom.

When Claude finally spotted Schloss Slobberchop in the distance, his stomach dropped, as if he had hit a patch of bad turbulence. He didn't know what to do, so he circled high above, out of sight and sound. The problem was that a map showed location, distance and direction, but not the physical reality of a place. On the map, Schloss Slobberchop sat on the riverside surrounded by patches of forest. In reality, a huge cliff face jutted up from the woods like a dark fang. Perched on top of this precipice was the Schloss, teetering on the edge of the cliff top hundreds of metres above the river.

The Schloss itself was tall, like a big slab. From above, it looked like an elongated cross with jagged towers and battlements and chimney-pots dotted all over the roof. To make matters worse, the whole region was smothered in thick forest — there was no place to land! The ground at the base of the castle was crawling with patrols of Watchdogz. It seemed that the whole mission was impossible.

Then Claude had an idea. It would be a tricky manoeuvre and one wrong jiggle would spell death. If he was going to save Major Tom, he would need to be as outrageously daring as Major Tom — he would have to pull it off perfectly, without alerting the DOGZ and their keen sense of smell and hearing.

The moon slipped behind a blanket of clouds, throwing the landscape into darkness. The timing had to be now. Claude switched off the noisy engine. It spluttered out, like Syd when he coughed up a furball. Instantly the tubby little plane began to lose speed and Claude felt it waggle beneath him. The controls became unresponsive, as if he were suddenly flying a huge dead fish.

He pushed the joystick forward, pointing the nose at the ground. The plane picked up speed and Claude was able to control it again as the wings caught the air. Wind whistled through the struts and the altimeter spun like a mad top as the plane lost altitude. Claude swung the aircraft in a wide diving arc, until he was heading into a deadly nosedive — straight at the castle!

Closer and closer he rushed towards the huge stone building.

At the last second Claude yanked back on the joystick. The nose of the plane rose up, almost too far, but Claude had timed his run perfectly. The plane touched down on the roof of the Schloss, bunny-hopping a few times before he cranked on the brakes, and brought it to a standstill. He was just centimetres from running out of roof.

BOING   BOING

Luckily the enemy had not expected an intruder to come from the skies, so the roof was free of Watchdogz. Claude hoped his luck would hold for the dangerous mission ahead.

CHAPTER 8

Within minutes Claude had found a clever way to sneak into the castle, but that was the easy part. Next he had to find Major Tom without being caught. Fortunately, Claude had a few cat tricks up his sleeve.

The place was a maze of long corridors, with hundreds of doors coming off the sides. How was he ever going to find Major Tom in this place? It would take days just to check every room, and by then the Major may have been tortured into giving up all of CATs' secrets.

Claude turned in to a long hallway. From the far end came a yellow glow. As he got closer and closer he heard a slowly rising noise.

He popped his head around the
corner to find himself on a little
balcony overlooking a huge room.

There was a terrible racket of yapping
DOGZ. And the smell! Hundreds of DOGZ were
wearing headsets and turning dials, moving markers
on a huge table map, and bustling here and there
with papers and folders. This must be HQ for
DOGZ Control — the centre of their operations.

DOGZ special security forces were everywhere and heavily armed Rottweilers guarded the doors.

From the secrecy of his high balcony Claude peeped out and scanned the room. Then he saw Major Tom! The Major was being marched out of the control centre by two guards.

Claude slipped down to a lower balcony unseen, and followed the guards until they were well away from the control room. Then, as stealthily as a black cat on a moonless night, he sneaked ahead of the guards.

ALL HEEL

'Meow-zaki!' The guards came around a corner and were knocked flat by a flying furball swinging from the chandelier. They didn't know what had hit them.

MEOW-ZAKI

'What's all this?' asked a bewildered Major Tom.

'I'm Claude D'Bonair,' said Claude, holding out a paw. 'I'm here to rescue you.'

'Rescue *me?*' said Major Tom, looking a bit surprised. 'Well, I myself was just about to escape, but I suppose I can take you along as well.'

'Are you okay to walk?' asked Claude.

'Walk?' laughed Major Tom. 'I can run and pounce and dance, you impertinent young kit.'

'It's just that we were afraid the DOGZ would have tortured you.'

'Torture?' said the Major thoughtfully. 'Oh yes, got plenty of that. They pulled my tail. Rubbed my fur the wrong way. Dunked me in a bathtub. And the mongrels dangled a piece of wool in front of me, just out of reach — for a week!'

'Flying furballs, sir!' cursed Claude.

'Never fear young kit, they didn't get anything out of me. I would rather eat dog roll than tell them even my mother's birthday.'

Claude had to admit that Major Tom was amazingly brave.

'Well, we'd better get going before these guards wake up,' said Claude.

'Follow me,' said Major Tom, and they raced off down the maze of corridors. The Major seemed to know where he was going, but in no time they came to a dead end.

'Dang and blast,' growled Major Tom.

They could hear a barking ruckus coming their way through the corridor. The DOGZ must have found the two unconscious guards.

'In here,' said Claude, and they nipped into a side door. It was a windowless room with nothing in it except a big writing desk.

'Oh, brilliant thinking!' Major Tom said sarcastically.

They could hear the DOGZ coming closer and closer. It was too late to go back and look for another escape and, anyway, the DOGZ outnumbered them one hundred to one. Even with Major Tom's legendary heroics, they could never win.

Major Tom raised his paws in the air and waited for the DOGZ to burst in. Meanwhile Claude looked around frantically. He grabbed the writing desk and shoved it across the room to block the door. It wouldn't hold them for long.

'So now what?' said Tom.

Claude grinned. 'We go out the same way I came in.' He indicated a small fireplace that had been hidden behind the desk. 'Up the chimney.'

'How?'

Claude pointed to his winch-watch.

The chimney was just big enough to fit Major Tom and Claude side by side. Claude adjusted his winch-watch to 6 o'clock — that would give him 6 metres of wire — which Claude estimated was the distance to the top of the chimney stack. He pointed his winch-watch upwards and told Major Tom to hold on.

He pressed the button.

Nothing happened.

He pressed it again and again and again and again. Nothing happened.

'That must be one of C-for's gadgets,' scoffed Major Tom. Claude nodded. None of the old cat's inventions ever worked the way they

were supposed to.

In the end the two cats clambered up the chimney paw by paw.

'I remember a story about a little kitten who climbed up a chimney,' grinned Claude, his teeth flashing white, out of his sooty face. 'I think his name was Tom as well.'

Major Tom coughed black soot. 'Some daring escape this is. I'll never live it down.'

Eventually they flopped out of the chimney onto the rooftop. Both cats were coughing and spluttering like Manx's Morane-Saulnier BB. But as Claude got to his feet he got a shock.

'Going for walkies?' said a huge Rottweiler. He wore a commander's studded collar. He barked a few orders at his soldiers. They surrounded the two cats, who slowly raised their paws in the air. '*Howl* you get out of this one?' the commander laughed, and his soldiers howled with laughter too.

Then he saw the glittering watch on Claude's wrist. His face changed to a nasty leer. 'You're a bit *ruff* to be wearing such a nice watch. Sergeant Wolfgang likes what he sees.'

'No, you don't want that,' said Claude. 'It doesn't do anything special.'

'It matches my collar,' said Sergeant Wolfgang,

and he nabbed Claude's watch and put it on his own wrist. 'Except the time isn't 6 o'clock!' He wound the dial and pressed it in.

Instantly the winch-watch shot out its
barbed hook.

Wup Wup Wup Wup

It lodged into one of the nearby towers.
Sergeant Wolfgang stood looking dumbfounded
for a second before he was whipped off his feet and
sent flying across the rooftop as the winch reeled
him in. Claude sprang high into the air as Sergeant
Wolfgang swept past, collecting half of his soldiers

wup wup

and sending the rest sprawling. The DOGZ commander splattered flat against the tower with a bone-crunching **CRASH!**

In the confusion, Claude shouted 'Come on!' and hauled Major Tom with him. They raced over to Manx's plane, which was propped at the end of the roof.

Claude's young legs raced ahead, and he took one flying leap straight into the pilot's catpit. Major Tom huffed up a second later.

'Hey! I'm the Top Cat around here. I'll do the flying.'

Just then bullets started pinging off the stone battlements. The DOGZ had regrouped.

'Just get in and man the gun!' yelled Claude.

Major Tom leaped into the gunner's seat and let out a squeal. 'What the blazes is this?'

Claude spun around to find two stowaways poking their heads out of the gunner's pit. The whining noise he had heard on the journey hadn't been the engine. It had been Picklepurr and Wigglebum.

'What on earth are you two doing here? Manx is going to kill me!'

'Not if dey kill you fwirst,' said Wigglebum, pointing behind them.

The DOGZ were pounding for them now — and Claude realised that the plane was facing the wrong way. They needed to turn it around to take off!

Tom gave a quick spray of fire from the Lewis gun, sending the DOGZ diving for cover behind chimney stacks with their tails between their legs.

At the same time, the force of the gunfire jolted the plane forward. It teetered on the edge of the castle roof.

'Hold on to your guts!' yelled Claude. The front wheels popped over the ledge and the whole plane, with Claude and Wigglebum and Picklepurr and Major Tom inside, tumbled down the sheer castle wall.

'Wheeeeeeeeee!' squealed
Wigglebum and Picklepurr.

'Get down!' shouted Claude.

As the plane plummeted
downwards he caught
a glimpse of stunned
Watchdogz, with vacant eyes
and tongues lolling, at the
bottom of the Schloss as they
whizzed past. They continued to

fall down the cliff face towards the river. He could
hear Major Tom caterwauling behind him. Claude
had no time to worry about that. He pumped the
primer and flicked the ignition. He could only
hope that the passing air was enough to help
spin the propeller and start the engine. The river
zoomed up towards them.

The engine spluttered. Claude pumped the

primer again. It gave a cough. He pumped with all his might and the engine flooded with petrol. This time it burst into a fury of power. Huge tongues of flame erupted from the exhausts and the propeller spun wildly into action. Claude threw back his head and hauled on the joystick.

The good old Morane-Saulnier BB pulled up barely in time and skimmed across the surface of the river, so low it left a blast of water spray rising behind. But Claude wasn't in control yet.

VAOOOOM

In the blink of an eye the plane crossed the river and plunged into the dark forest lining the riverbank. It took all of Claude's skill and concentration as he weaved in and out of the black trunks that zoomed past.

In a flash they burst into a forest clearing, blazing with light. A DOGZ battalion was busy working on some complex machinery. They weren't expecting a CATs fighter plane to plough out of the trees.

DOGZ leaped for their lives, and Claude rolled and twirled the plane to avoid the cranes and wires.

Gunfire cracked behind them as the Watchdogz took aim — but now Claude was in control. He lifted the nose and they popped clear of the treetops.

He turned and began to follow the river back to safety, and home.

Wigglebum couldn't stop jiggling and bobbing, she was so excited to be flying. Picklepurr kept poking and fiddling with everything, asking, 'Claude, what does this do? Claude, what happens if I pull this? Claude, what does that dial mean? Claude, what's that plane over there?'

'What plane?' said Claude, looking around frantically.

'That plane, silly. The big red one.'

The sound of machine guns ripped the air from above. Claude looked up to his left as a squadron of dogfighters emerged from behind a cloud.

'Get down girls!' Claude yelled.
'Tom! 10 o'clock!'

'What?' said Major Tom, looking at his watch. 'It's almost 4 in the morning old chap.'

'No!' yelled Claude. '10 o'clock — the direction — up to our left. Incoming fighters!'

The attackers swooped down with a burst of fire and Claude rolled the plane to the right. Bullets whizzed past, missing them by a whisker.

The attackers looped around in a tight formation as they lined up for another run. With dread, Claude noticed the markings on the lead plane.

'What does K9 mean?' asked Wiggle.

'It means we're in trouble,' gulped Claude. 'It's The Red Setter.'

Not far ahead the black forest ended, and Claude saw a pitted grey strip of earth that was the no man's land between the front lines. If he could just make it back to CATs territory they would be safe.

The enemy fighters lined up for another shot, but this time Claude and Major Tom were prepared. With an experienced aviator like Major Tom in the gun seat, the enemy didn't stand a chance.

The Major opened fire with the Lewis,
sweeping the machine-gun along
the enemy formation.

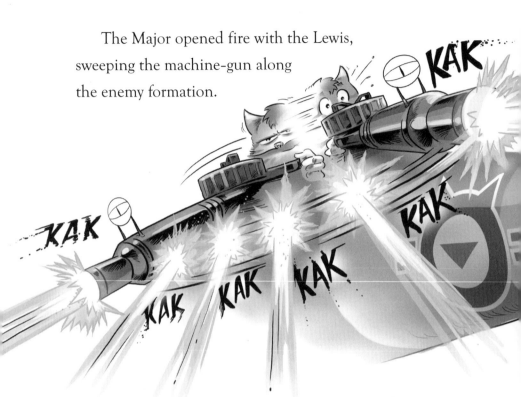

Suddenly the little plane lurched to one side.

'What happened?' Claude called back.

'Umm, ah . . . our tail's
been hit by machine-gun fire,'
Major Tom said sheepishly.

He did not explain exactly
whose machine-gun fire.

'I can't keep her in the air!' yelled Claude.

The plane toppled towards the treetops. Up
ahead the forest ended at the barren no man's land.
They were now roaring above the DOGZ trenches.

Enemy fire was coming from above and below, popping holes of starlight through the wings. The plane was losing power. The wheels skimmed the muddy rim of a bomb crater before snagging on a barrier of barbed wire. The plane began to pivot in the air. For a split second Claude saw the faces of CATs soldiers in the trenches below — they'd crossed into home territory. Then the machine was rolling end-over-end in a mad cartwheel.

SPR-OING

They came to a halt in a huge crater
filled with muddy water.

KER-SPLASH!

Claude woke up. He must have been knocked out.
That was close, Claude thought. *Surely one of my nine
lives is gone.* Then he remembered little Wiggle and
Pickle! He looked around frantically, but he couldn't
see the kittens in the wreckage.

Then he heard them.

'Wheeeee!' Wigglebum and Picklepurr were
sliding down the muddy crater and splashing into
the pond at the bottom. When they saw Claude,
they cried, 'We thought you were having a catnap, so
we decided not to wake you. Can we do that again?'

Thank goodness! sighed Claude. If anything had

happened to them he couldn't have faced Manx, especially not after she had already lost her parents. In the distance he could hear a CATs medic crew coming to their assistance. He checked Major Tom, who was semi-conscious in the back of the wreck. They were bruised, but at least he had rescued Major Tom and brought them all home safe and sound.

mee-ow
mee-ow
mee-ow
mee-ow

'You're lucky to be alive, mate,' said Syd.

Claude was propped up in a hospital bed with his head wrapped in bandages. 'It's just a minor concussion,' he complained. 'Get me back in the air.'

'Surely it's not *all* bad?' Syd winked, as one of the nurses came over.

'Urrrgh,' said Claude. 'They're the worst part!'

'Yoo-hoo, Claude darling,' called out nurse
Sinja, mincing down the line of
beds. 'Look what *I've* got.'

Sinja came over excitedly
waving a newspaper.

'Sydney!' she growled. 'We can't have that filthy
habit in a hospital.'

'Sorry,' said Syd, taking his boots off the bed.

'Not that,' said Claude. 'She means your puffing
on that disgusting catnip.'

Nurse Sinja turned to Claude with the intense
focus of a lighthouse beam and flapped the newspaper in his face. 'Guess who's in the newsy-woosy!'

TUESDAY 5 JUNE

Hero Flies Free

Our intrepid war reporter Fifi Hackles reveals how a dashing young pilot made a daring escape from the clutches of the DOGZ.

While kittens across the katdom were snuggled safe in their beds, dashing young pilot Major Ginger Tom (who is no stranger to our readers) was making a daring raid on DOGZ HQ. At one point the Major was surrounded by a squad of crack DOGZ soldiers, but he managed to single-handedly fight his way to freedom. 'I simply commanded them to sit, lie down, and play dead,' Major Tom said of his escape, laughing off his bravery.

The Major was later seen leaving the swanky London nightclub Meow! He told this reporter not to worry, as he would soon be in the skies again defending the katdom. He did mention one special cat that he couldn't have done all this without. 'I'd like to thank my mother for always being my biggest fan,' he said.

CAT BURGLAR BEHIND BARS

A dog who took advantage of harmless
... behind bars

Post

EDITOR IN CHIEF D. MURRAY. PUBLISHED BY CHAPMAN & CO. SINCE 1822

MEOW!

HEROIC FIGHTER PILOT MAJOR TOM SEEMED TO HAVE RECOVERED FROM HIS ESCAPE ORDEAL.

DOG ROYALS
MISSING

Dethroned King Charles and his family have not been seen since DOGZ troops invaded the royal palace in Berlin. There are rumours that the King has been impounded by DOGZ leader Alf Alpha.

READ MORE
ON PAGE 9.

All new *Catillac Sport*

SKI
Switzerland

KIPPERS
5 Francs per dozen

Smokey's Fish

'Flying furballs!' growled Claude.

'I know,' swooned nurse Sinja. 'Isn't Major Tom just the cat's pyjamas!'

'What's all this?' asked Syd.

Claude flung him the paper.

'Crikey dingo!' spluttered Syd, almost choking on his pipe. 'Have you seen what it says?!'

'They didn't even mention my name,' muttered Claude.

'Not that,' grinned Syd. 'Look. Kippers! Only five francs a dozen!'

Claude rolled his eyes and gazed out
the window at the beautiful blue sky. He
gave a little grin, knowing that Commander
Snookums had recommended him for a
Purple Paw — the highest medal for bravery.

With any luck Manx would have his plane Kitty
Hawk fixed soon and he'd be flying high in action
once again. As long as DOGZ like The Red Setter
were out there, none of them were safe.

Claude had a feeling that they hadn't had their
last dogfight.

C. D'BONAIR

Donovan Bixley is one of New Zealand's most recognisable picture book creators, with numerous awards and accolades to his name. His books have been published in 25 countries, and his part-comic — part-novel *Monkey Boy* was selected by the International Youth Library as one of the top 200 children's books in the world.

Some of the interesting things he has illustrated include Shelob making Kentucky Fried Frodo, Mozart telling fart jokes and a veloci-rapping dinosaur.

Find out more about Donovan and his work at www.donovanbixley.com